Officially Noted

pen marks on plastic foldover

8/25/07 DS

Tap-Dance Fever

by **Pat Brisson**

Illustrated by **Nancy Cote**

Boyds Mills Press

With love for my mother-in-law, Irene Brisson,
sweet and sassy and 95 years young
    —*P. B.*

To all my friends in the F.A.N.
(www.freelanceartistsnetwork.com)
who keep me inspired.
    —*N. C.*

Text copyright © 2005 by Pat Brisson
Illustrations copyright © 2005 by Nancy Cote
All rights reserved

Published by Boyds Mills Press, Inc.
A Highlights Company
815 Church Street
Honesdale, Pennsylvania 18431
Printed in China
Visit our Web site at www.boydsmillspress.com

Library of Congress Cataloging-in-Publication Data

Brisson, Pat.
  Tap-dance fever / by Pat Brisson ; illustrated by Nancy Cote.— 1st ed.
      p. cm.
Summary: Annabelle Applegate will not stop tap-dancing no matter
what the frustrated citizens of Fiddler's Creek do to make her quit.
ISBN 1-59078-290-9
[1. Tap dancing—Fiction.] I. Cote, Nancy, ill. II. Title.

PZ7.B78046Tap 2004   [E]—dc22
2004014575

First edition, 2005
The text is set in 15-point Minion.
The illustrations are done in watercolor and gouache.

10 9 8 7 6 5 4 3 2 1

ANNABELLE APPLEGATE was the tap-dancingest girl in
Fiddler's Creek. She danced so much she wore out the linoleum in her
ma's kitchen. She made ridges along Creek Road on her way to school.
She even danced a hole clear through the rickety old schoolhouse
floor. Folks asked her to stop, but it did no good. Annabelle only heard
the song in her head that made her feet want to move. No doubt about
it—she had Tap-Dance Fever and it wouldn't let her go.

"Something must be done!" declared her teacher, Mrs. Hagglehorn. She called an emergency meeting at the schoolhouse that very evening.

"She's a nuisance!" cried Mrs. Ethel Pontoon. "My chickens refuse to lay because she dances past my farm every morning."

"She's a danger!" shouted Mrs. Hagglehorn. "Look at the hole she danced through this floor."

"She's a hazard!" said Harville T. Stone. "When I hit that ridge she danced into Creek Road, I blew a tire on my truck and busted up my glasses."

"Well," said Mayor Peachtree. "What should we do?"
Everyone thought for a minute.
"Maybe if we put enough dance-defyin' stuff in her
way, she'll get frustrated and forget all about it," said
Harville T. Stone.

Folks figured it was worth a try. They ran home, got all the toe-stubbing, ankle-twisting paraphernalia they could find, and dumped it along Creek Road. They thought that would be the end of it.

But the next morning along came Annabelle tappity, tap, tapping down Creek Road. She looked at the mess left by the townsfolk, then tippy tapped carefully forward. It was slow going at first, but finally she slappity-skipped and tippity-hopped over every bit of that foot-bustin' heap of refuse (and invented a few new steps in the process). She arrived at school just as the bell rang and danced through the rest of the day.

That night the townsfolk met again.
"We need another idea," said Mayor Peachtree.
"Take away her dance shoes!" cried Mrs. Ethel Pontoon.
Everyone agreed. Deputy Thistledown was sent to get Annabelle's beloved tap shoes. People were convinced their worries were over.

But the next morning along came Annabelle tappity-tap . . . skippity-slap . . . tippity-hopping down Creek Road—bottle caps nailed to the bottoms of a pair of her daddy's old work boots.

"Is this mess still here?" she asked in surprise.

Spying a dump truck down the road, she got an idea. Slappity, hop, *kick!* Tappity, slide, *kick!* Tappity, hop . . . slappity, slide . . . shuffle, step, *kick!* She soon kicked every bit of dance-defyin' refuse smack dab into the back of that truck. Having done her civic duty (and invented some new steps), Annabelle danced through the rest of the day.

That night a frustrated group of townsfolk met again.
"What do we do *now*?" asked Mayor Peachtree.
"Take away her work boots!" declared Mrs. Hagglehorn.
Everyone agreed and Deputy Thistledown was sent off again.
Surely their problem was over now.

But the next morning along came Annabelle shuffle, step, tappity, tappity . . . heel, toe, tappity, tappity . . . shuffling left, shuffling right all along Creek Road—pennies taped to the bottoms of her bare feet. Passing Mrs. Ethel Pontoon's farm— heel, toe, tappity, tappity . . . heel, toe, tappity, tappity—she heard an unexpected *hissss*. Though stunned to see dozens of rattlesnakes in her path, she couldn't keep her feet still. Tappity. *Rattle*. Tappity. *Rattle*. Tappity, tappity, tap. *Rattle, rattle, hissss.*

Annabelle couldn't believe it—they were dancing right along with her! Knowing better than to take rattlesnakes to school, she led them to the stage at the empty fairgrounds farther along Creek Road, where curious passersby stopped to watch. Before the day was over, folks from six surrounding counties had heard of Annabelle Applegate and her Tap-Dancing Rattlesnakes (and she'd invented even more new steps).

Changes were fast and furious after that. Annabelle set up a regular schedule of performances and charged admission. With so much traffic on Creek Road, the county decided to pave it. Annabelle's tap-dancing ridges were gone forever.

Tourist money poured into town. The rickety old schoolhouse floor was replaced. Mrs. Hagglehorn, who'd secretly longed for a career in the theater, designed a red-spangled costume for Annabelle to wear in the show and sold tickets at weekend performances.

Mrs. Ethel Pontoon finally realized the rattlesnakes, not
Annabelle, were causing her chickens to stop laying. With
them gone, her chickens produced like never before, so she
opened a stand to sell the extras.

Harville T. Stone, in his new glasses, looked so debonair that a certain local widow invited him to dinner and baked his favorite pie. He convinced her to go into the pie-selling business with him.

With her earnings, Annabelle replaced the linoleum in her ma's kitchen and built a dance studio where she offered lessons to anyone with a hankerin' to learn.

The whole town came to her Open House. When they ran
out of small talk, someone called out, "Dance for us, Annabelle!"
Annabelle tapped to center stage, took a deep breath, and
smiled broadly.
"I'd be happy to," she said at last.

And Annabelle Applegate danced straight on till morning.